WS

Rockets

LITTLE T

The Royal Roar

Raaaar!

Frank Rodgers

A & C Black • London

Rockets series:

CROOK CATCHERS - Karen Wallace & Judy Brown

HAUNTED MOUSE - Dee Shulman

LITTLE T - Frank Rodgers

MOTLEY'S CREW - Margaret Ryan & Margaret Chamberlain

MR CROC - Frank Rodgers

MRS MAGIC - Wendy Smith

MY FUNNY FAMILY - Colin West

ROVER - Chris Powling & Scoular Anderson

SILLY SAUSAGE - Michaela Morgan & Dee Shulman

WIZARD'S BOY - Scoular Anderson

First paperback edition 2002
First published 2002 in hardback by A & C Black (Publishers) Ltd
37 Soho Square, London W1D 3QZ

Text and illustrations copyright © 2002 Frank Rodgers

The right of Frank Rodgers to be identified as author
and illustrator of this work has been asserted by him
in accordance with the Copyright, Designs and Patents Act 1988.

ISBN 0-7136-6052-X

A CIP catalogue record for this book is available
from the British Library.

Printed and bound by G. Z. Printek, Bilbao, Spain.

Chapter One

Little Prince
T Rex was
proud of
his dad.

A lot of kings do boring things.
They read speeches or watch parades.
Not Little T's dad.

Every year King High T the Mighty
roared a Royal Roar.

RAAAR!

It rattled the tiles on
the Royal Roof...

...it rattled the
crockery in the
Royal Kitchen...

...and it rattled the false teeth in the
Royal Old Dinosaurs' Home.

It was a special day and all the dinosaurs loved it.

It was going to happen at two o'clock the next day and they were all prepared.

Chess-piece ear plugs

Chess-piece ear plugs
the perfect gift!

The Royal Earplug Factory had been doing roaring business...

...the Royal Hat shop had sold out of novelty crash-helmets...

...and the Royal String Works had made Super-String for tying everything down.

Little T was excited.
'One day I'll do the Royal Roar,
won't I, Dad?' he said.
His dad grinned.
'Yes,' he replied.

When you're grown up.

I'm going to start practising now!

'I'll soon be as good as you,' said Little T.
'Just you wait. Everyone will be surprised!'

Chapter Two

Everyone was surprised. Because even though Little T's roar wasn't very loud he did it in the oddest places.

Raaaaar!

He roared up the chimney...

Eeek!

...and surprised the Royal Sweep.

Raaaar!

He roared in the pantry...

Uuuh!

...and surprised the Royal Cook.

He roared in the bathroom...

...and surprised his mum.

'Little T!' cried Queen Teena. 'You've given me goose pimples!'

But Little T enjoyed roaring.
It was too much fun to stop.

He roared
outside the
Royal Nursery...

...and surprised his sister...

He roared into
the sentry-box...

Raaaaar!

...and surprised
the Royal Guards.

He roared down a hole...

Raaaar!

...and surprised
the Royal
Drain-layers.

Everyone was getting a bit fed up but
Little T was having fun.

Beside the pond in the park he met his
friends, Don, Bron, Tops and Dinah.

Dinah was holding a megaphone.
Her dad, the Royal Park-Keeper, used it
to shout to the boats on the pond.

'Aha!' exclaimed Little T.

Just the thing to make my roar louder!

He borrowed the megaphone and climbed onto a bench.
'Listen to this!' he said.

You'll be surprised!

He took a deep breath.
His friends stuck their fingers in their ears.

Chapter Three

Just then, King High T the Mighty came round the corner. He was out for his daily stroll.

Little T roared right into his ear.

Raaaar!

Ahhhhh!

High T got such a fright that he leapt sideways...

SPLASH!

...straight into the pond.

Spluttering and gasping, King High T
the Mighty crawled back onto the bank.
He was soaking wet.

Little T had roared one roar too many.
'Oops! Sorry, Dad!' he cried.

I didn't see you.

High T was not amused. His teeth were
chattering.

N...n...no more
r...r...roaring,
Little T !

Shivering, he trudged off back to the
castle to get dry.
The dinosaurs were sorry that the king
had got wet.

But they were
pleased that
Little T wouldn't
give them any
more nasty
surprises.

Next morning it was Little T's turn to get
a surprise.
His dad had caught a terrible cold.

His Royal Nose
was red and he
had a scarf
wrapped
round his
Royal Neck.

'I've lost my voice, Little T,' he croaked
sadly.

The Royal Roar
will have to be
cancelled.

Little T felt miserable. He had spoiled
the special day for everyone.

He moped
around feeling
sorry for himself.

19

Then he had a great idea.
'Why don't I do the Royal Roar,
Dad?' he cried.

I could use the
park-keeper's
megaphone!

His dad shook his head.
'Your roar is too small,' he croaked.

And so is the
megaphone.

Little T thought hard.

'What if I got a bigger megaphone, Dad?' he said. 'That would make my roar loud enough.'

Wouldn't it?

His dad looked doubtful.

'It might,' he croaked. 'But I don't know if the dinosaurs would like it.'

They've had enough of your surprises.

But Little T was desperate to make amends.

'Why don't we give it a try, Dad?' he said.

His dad looked even more doubtful.

Pleeeeease!

High T sighed and nodded.
'All right,' he croaked.

Chapter Four

Little T rushed off and told his friends about his plan.

They searched for a big megaphone but couldn't find one anywhere.
So they decided to make one themselves.

They collected
drain pipes
from the Royal
Plumber...

...armour from the
Royal Blacksmith...

...a hose from the
Royal Gardener...

...and they found a big old, dusty funnel
in the Royal Attic.

25

They took all the bits and pieces to the
Royal Balcony and set to work.

'We'll have to hurry!' cried Little T.

The minutes ticked towards two o'clock but at last it was finished.

With its pipes and tubes it was the biggest megaphone in the world!

There was no time to test it.
It was two o'clock and all the dinosaurs
were ready and waiting.

Earplugs were in, chin-straps were
buckled and children were tied to their
parents' legs for safety.

King High T the Mighty appeared on the
Royal Balcony.

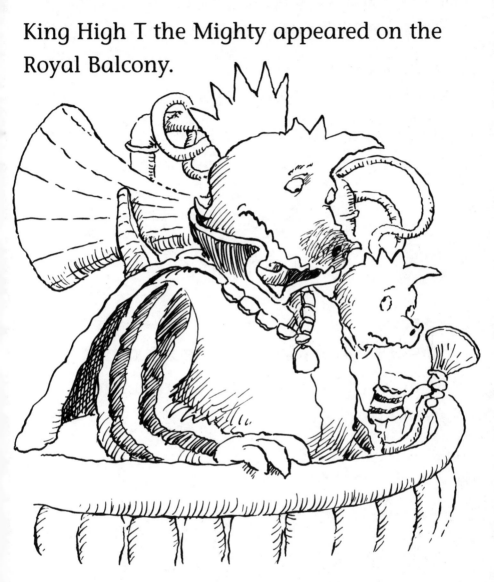

The dinosaurs cheered but High T was
worried. He didn't know if they would
like his change of plan.

He held up his hands and the dinosaurs
fell silent.

'Today,' he croaked, 'the Royal Roar will
be done by my son,
Little T.'

The dinosaurs looked at each other.
They could hardly hear him because of
the earplugs.

The dinosaurs cheered again.

Good old High T !!

High T was surprised.
'They don't seem to mind,' he said to
Little T.

Little T
grinned.

Here goes,
then !

Little T roared his little roar into the megaphone.

It shot up the hosepipe...

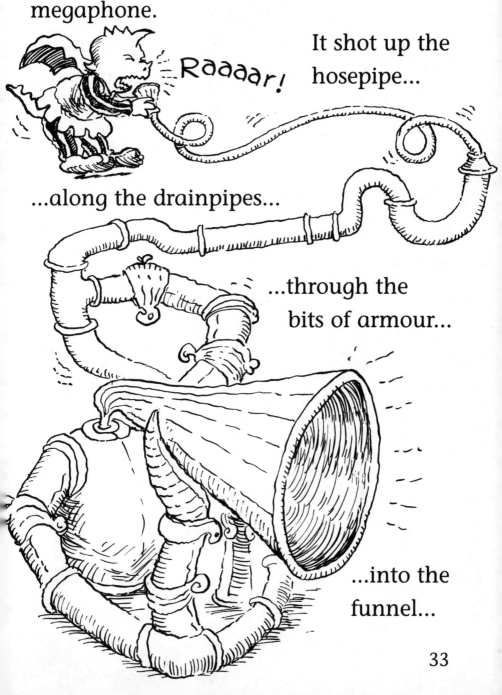

Raaaar!

...along the drainpipes...

...through the bits of armour...

...into the funnel...

...and stopped.

Nothing came out.

The crowd looked at the king and then at one another.
What was going on?

On the Royal Balcony the king looked at Little T anxiously.

'What's wrong?' he croaked.

'The roar got stuck in the pipes, Dad,' hissed Little T.

I'll try again!

High T turned and smiled sheepishly at the crowd.

Chapter Five

Once more Little T roared his little roar into the megaphone.

Once more it shot up the hosepipe...

Raaaar!

...along the drainpipes...

...through the bits of armour...

...into the funnel...

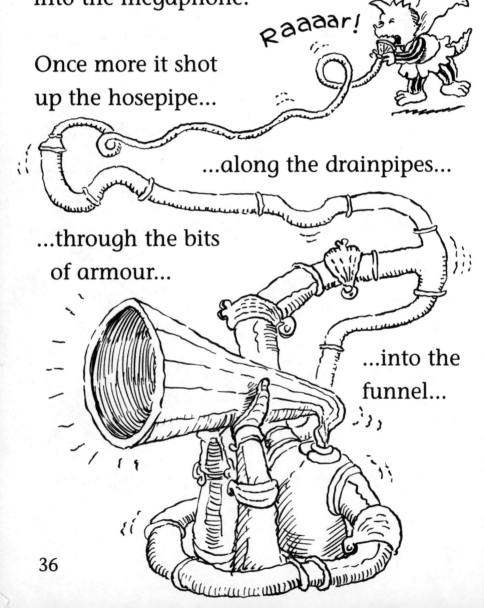

...and once more it stopped.

The crowd stared at the king.
Why didn't he roar?

Up on the Royal Balcony Little T stuck his head inside the funnel.

'Oh no!' he gasped. 'There's an old nest in here! It's full of twigs and feathers.'

That's what stopped the roar!

38

High T leaned on the funnel to look
inside and...

...the megaphone
fell apart.

'Oops,' croaked High T.

Now what will we do?

The crowd was becoming restless.
What was delaying the Royal Roar?

Suddenly Little T
had another idea.
Reaching into the
funnel he grabbed
a feather.

He stuck it under his dad's
nose and wiggled it.
High T's big nose
twitched.

Little T wiggled the feather some more.

'Ah...' gurgled High
T, his mouth
beginning to open.

'Ah,' said the crowd.
'At last.'

This could be it!

'Ah... Ah...' gurgled
High T, his mouth
opening wider.

'Aha!' cried the crowd. 'Yes, it could.'

High T started to tremble.

He gripped hold of
the balcony with
both hands.

He began to shake.

His eyes closed, his head went back and his mouth opened as wide as a cave.

'Ah...' he went.

Ah... Ah...
Ah....
Ah.....

CHAAAR!

High T roared out such a sneeze he nearly blew his own head off.

The mighty, roaring sneeze swept over the dinosaurs.

The knights' suits of armour fell apart...

...the cook's cakes collapsed...

...and the wigs of the dinosaurs-in-waiting were blasted off at a hundred miles an hour.

'Wow!' cried the crowd. 'What a Royal Roar! The best ever! Worth all the waiting.'

What a dinosaur! What a king!

High T blushed with pride.
'Smart thinking, Little T,' he said in
a croaky whisper. 'You saved
the day.'

Shame about the megaphone.

'It's all right, Dad,' replied Little T with a
grin. 'I'll fix it. And when I do I'll roar
the loudest roar you've ever heard.'

You'll be
surprised!

'No more surprises!' cried Don, Bron,
Tops and Dinah.

Quickly they lifted up the big funnel
and put it over him.

We're not going
to let you out
unless you promise
to stop roaring.

Out of the top of the funnel came Little
T's echoing voice.
'I promise I'll stop roaring.'

His friends lifted off the funnel and Little
T grinned.
'I'll do something else instead,' he said.